Shai & Emmie

STAR IN

To my family, friends, and fans,
for the love and continuous support
—Q. W.

To Janet Giewont, the best teacher in the universe. Thank
you for bringing love and light to our family.
—N. E. O.

For my niece, Emma
—S. M.

SIMON & SCHUSTER BOOKS FOR YOUNG READERS
An imprint of Simon & Schuster Children's Publishing Division
1230 Avenue of the Americas, New York, New York 10020

Text copyright © 2018 by Jarece Productions, Inc.
Illustration copyright © 2018 by Sharee Miller

For information about special discounts for bulk purchases, please contact Simon & Schuster Special Sales at 1-866-506-1949 or business@simonandschuster.com.
The Simon & Schuster Speakers Bureau can bring authors to your live event. For more information or to book an event, contact the Simon & Schuster Speakers Bureau at 1-866-248-3049 or visit our website at www.simonspeakers.com.
Book design by Chloë Foglia
The text for this book was set in Bembo.
The illustrations for this book were rendered in watercolor and ink.
Manufactured in the United States of America / 1217 FFG
First Edition
2 4 6 8 10 9 7 5 3 1
Library of Congress Cataloging-in-Publication Data
Names: Wallis, Quvenzhané, 2003– author. | Ohlin, Nancy, author. | Miller, Sharee (Illustrator), illustrator.
Title: Shai & Emmie star in Dancy pants! / Quvenzhané Wallis with Nancy Ohlin ; illustrated by Sharee Miller.
Other titles: Shai and Emmie star in Dancy pants! | Dancy pants!
Description: First edition. | New York : Simon & Schuster Books for Young Readers, 2018. | Series: A Shai & Emmie story ; 2 | Summary: Third-grader Shai, paired with her best friend Emmie and classmate Rio in a major dance competition, makes a bet with her rival, Gabby, and then must push Emmie to win.
Identifiers: LCCN 2016059113 (print) | LCCN 2017029049 (ebook) | ISBN 9781481458856 (hardback) | ISBN 9781481458870 (eBook)
Subjects: | CYAC: Dance—Fiction. | Contests—Fiction. | Friendship—Fiction. | Schools—Fiction. | Family life—Fiction. | African Americans—Fiction. | BISAC: JUVENILE FICTION / Performing Arts / General. | JUVENILE FICTION / Social Issues / Friendship. | JUVENILE FICTION / Readers / Chapter Books.
Classification: LCC PZ7.1.W357 (ebook) | LCC PZ7.1.W357 Shm 2018 (print) | DDC [Fic]—dc23
LC record available at https://lccn.loc.gov/2016059113

Shai & Emmie

STAR IN

Quvenzhané Wallis

WITH Nancy Ohlin   ILLUSTRATED BY Sharee Miller

Simon & Schuster Books for Young Readers
NEW YORK   LONDON   TORONTO   SYDNEY   NEW DELHI

Also by Quvenzhané Wallis

Shai & Emmie Star in Break an Egg!

Program

SCENE 1

Hurricane Shai

"You are hurricanes!" Ms. Englert called out to the class.

Shai Williams pretended to be a hurricane. She spun around and around and waved her arms in a swirly pattern. She made whooshing wind noises through her lips.

Nearby, her best friend, Emmie, did some tiptoe-y ballet steps.

"Are you raindrops?" Shai asked Emmie.

"Yes, exactly!" Emmie replied.

Shai swooped in wide circles around Emmie, spinning and arm waving and whooshing. Emmie quickened her raindrop steps until they were a frenzied staccato: *plinkplinkplinkplink-plink*. The two girls were a hurricane together!

"Now the storm is starting to wind down . . . down . . . down," said Ms. Englert in a hushed voice.

All the students began winding down, down, down. Shai stopped spinning and arm waving and whooshing. Emmie's raindrops slowed to a trickle.

"Oh, look! The sun is coming out!" Ms. Englert exclaimed.

Shai tipped her face to the sky—or rather, the ceiling of the dance studio—and made flappy jazz hands. Emmie did the same. They smiled sunny smiles at each other.

Ms. Englert clapped, and everyone came to

a halt. "That was lovely. No, not just lovely . . . magnificent! Now we're going to pretend we are salads!"

Salads?

Ms. Englert was the dance teacher at the Sweet Auburn School for the Performing Arts. She was full of zany ideas. Today she was having each student improvise, or make up, dances to go with different themes.

Shai loved Ms. Englert. She also loved the dance studio, which was on the second floor of the school. It had mirrored walls and ballet barres. It had framed photographs of famous dancers like Alvin Ailey, Savion Glover, and Misty Copeland. It had a poster of three dancing honeybees that said: BEE AMAZING!

☆ 3 ☆

After the salad dance, Ms. Englert had the class improvise a crayon dance. (Shai improvised her favorite color, turquoise.) Then a video-game dance. (She improvised Olimar from her favorite game, *Pikmin* for Wii U.)

It was time for a break. The students got their water bottles. Ms. Englert played some relaxing chirping-birds music on her phone. She sat down on her big blue yoga ball.

"So I'd like to put something out there." Ms. Englert fluttered her fingers and traced three squiggly letters in the air. "*D* . . . *W* . . . *K* . . . Does anyone know what that abbreviation stands for?"

Shai made a scrunchy thinking face. *D* and *W* and *K*.

Decorating With Kites?

Driving While Karaoking?

Shai's friend Rio raised his hand. "DWK stands for Dancing With Kids. It's a dance competition!"

"Yes, Rio. Exactly! It's held in a different city each year. This year it will be right here in Atlanta, at the Robinson Arena," said Ms. Englert.

Oh yeah. Shai had seen the competition on TV once, and the dancers had been really amazetastic!

"Are we going to DWK for a field trip?" a boy named Capone asked Ms. Englert.

"Even better! I was thinking that we could enter the competition as a class!" Ms. Englert replied.

Shai's jaw dropped. *Enter the competition as a class?* Ms. Englert might as well have said, "Let's enter the Olympics as a class!" or "Let's fly to

Jupiter as a class!" They were only third graders. Granted, Dancing With Kids was just for
kids. But from the one time Shai had watched
it, the competitors had seemed like the best
dancers in the universe, practically.

Also, the Robinson Arena was hunormous!
Shai glanced out the window. There it was . . .
stretching across Atlanta's downtown skyline
like a silver spaceship. Momma and Daddy had
taken the family there for the women's basketball

championship, and there had been a billion zillion people in the audience.

The dance studio filled with buzzy, excited whispers. Emmie raised one eyebrow at Shai. It was one of Emmie's new skills, raising one eyebrow, and it made her look like a cool mad scientist. Shai tried to raise one eyebrow back, but her eyebrow wouldn't cooperate, so she ended up squinting and squishing her cheeks instead. Emmie giggled.

"What's the grand prize? Is it lots and lots of money?" Gabby spoke up. Gabby was Shai's frenemy, which was friend plus enemy.

Ms. Englert shifted on her yoga ball. "Well . . . I'm not sure. But we're not doing this for money or ribbons or anything like that. We're doing this so you can get valuable competition experience— and also have a good time! There's nothing like being under the bright lights on a big stage!"

"I bet it's like a hundred dollars. Or maybe even a thousand dollars," Gabby murmured to a girl named Isabella. Gabby was kind of a know-it-all.

Shai sipped at her water bottle. She had been in only one other dance competition before. Four years ago her class from the Twinkle Toes Dance Studio had participated in a local competition at the community center. They had performed a shuffly tap routine to the song "I Wish" from *Happy Feet*. It had been super-scary, especially when Shai forgot her Mumble solo steps and had to improvise new ones on the spot. But it had been super-fun, too, and their group had come in fifth place. They had received a plaque and gift certificates for ice-cream cones at the Scoop.

But that wasn't the same as competing in Dancing With Kids.

And the community center wasn't the same as the Robinson Arena.

Not even close.

Were Shai and her classmates ready for the challenge?

The Cupcake Bet

Ms. Englert handed out the list of dance routines they would be performing for Dancing With Kids. The competition was next month.

"Singin' in the Rain" (tap): Shai, Rio, and Emmie

"Dance of the Flowers" (ballet): Ezra, Nya, and Sarah

"It's the Hard-Knock Life" (contemporary): Ruby, Ben,
   and Capone

"I Wish" (tap): Gabby, Isabella, and Jay

"Over the Rainbow" (ballet): Libby, Nick, and Julia

"Circle of Life" (contemporary): Glenn, Garrett, and Molly

Ms. Englert had added lots of smiley faces and hearts and stars, too.

No one was performing a solo. "I want everyone to work in teams, support each other, and not stress out," Ms. Englert told the class. "The theme here is fun, boys and girls. F–U–N, *fun!*"

At lunch Shai and Emmie sat at their usual table in the cafeteria by the potted palm tree and discussed the dance assignments. Wednesday was Chinese Bang-Bang Chicken day, which was their favorite menu item for the whole entire week, especially since Becky the cafeteria lady had a special way of making the chicken with double-triple-quadruple extra sauce. Along with the chicken, Shai had two regular milks, like she always did, and Emmie had one chocolate milk, like she always did.

"I'm so *delighted* we're doing a dance together!" Shai said.

"Yes, it's quite *splendid*," Emmie replied.

Shai and Emmie were reading *Little Women* for the Cool Books Club, which was their new book club. They were the only members so far. "Delighted" and "splendid" were *Little Women* words.

Shai was also delighted that she was in one of the tap groups. The students at the school all studied tap, ballet, modern, contemporary, hip-hop, lyrical, and other styles. Tap was Shai's favorite.

Also, Emmie was an amazetastic tap dancer, and so was Rio. They both wanted to be professional dancers when they grew up.

Shai spotted Rio searching for a table. She waved to him.

"Would you care to join Emmie and me for *luncheon*?" she called out.

"Luncheon? Um, sure!" Rio replied.

He sat down at the girls' table and dug into his food. "So when do you guys want to start rehearsing 'Singin' in the Rain'?" he asked with a mouth full of chicken.

"Well, Ms. Englert said she'd be teaching us our choreography this week. So maybe we could start this weekend?" Emmie suggested.

Shai blew bubbles in her milk, which she wasn't allowed to do at home for some reason. "We could take turns rehearsing at each other's houses," she said in a gurgly, bubbly voice.

Rio frowned. "Um, yeah . . . I'll have to ask my mom and dad. Our house is kind of small."

"Okay. Why don't we have the first rehearsal at my house, then? This Saturday afternoon?" said Shai.

Rio and Emmie nodded. Shai made a mental note to herself: *Ask Momma and Daddy if we can use the basement for our rehearsal.* Among other things, that would mean telling Jamal, Samantha, Jacobe, and all the dogs and cats to KEEP OUT. Especially Samantha, who could be a pesty pest sometimes. Actually, *all* the time.

"What should we call our trio?" Emmie asked.

"How about the Dancy Pants Trio?" Rio

suggested. "You know, like fancy-pants, except with a *D*?"

"Delightful!" said Shai.

"Splendid!" said Emmie.

After lunch Shai headed to her locker, humming happily. She was really glad to be in the Dancy Pants Trio with her friends. It was going to be so much fun!

When she opened her locker door, a bunch of items tumbled out: sheet music, drama scripts, textbooks, fruity markers, and her apple and cheese stick snack from . . . last month? *Oops.* She stuffed it all back in and pulled out her clarinet case for her orchestra music class.

Gabby pranced up to her. She was wearing a T-shirt with a big gold movie-star star on it. Her family used to live in Hollywood, California. She considered herself to be a Real Actress because she had been in a toothpaste commercial and a movie called *The Attack of the Zombie Potatoes 4*.

"Hi, Shane!" Gabby sang.

"Oh, hey Grabby."

"Shane" and "Grabby" were their nicknames for each other. When they had first met, Gabby kept pretending that she had forgotten Shai's name and called her "Shane." And Shai had thought "Grabby" was a fitting nickname for Gabby, who wanted everything for herself. But now they got along, sort of.

The truth was, Shai still wasn't sure if she liked Gabby or not.

Gabby leaned against the locker next to Shai's.

"*Soooo* . . . I guess you and Emmie and Rio are doing a tap routine for the competition?"

"Yup. I guess you and Isabella and Jay are too."

"Wanna make it interesting?" Gabby said with a sly smile.

"Interesting . . . how?" Shai asked.

"If my team gets a ribbon in the tap-dancing category and yours doesn't, you have to bring me a cupcake every day for a whole week. And the same if your team gets a ribbon. Deal?"

Shai hesitated. "But Ms. Englert said we're not supposed to worry about ribbons and stuff. We're supposed to have F-U-N."

"This *will* be F-U-N. It will be an F-U-N B-E-T," Gabby spelled.

A fun bet? Shai considered this.

"No, thanks," she said after a moment. She didn't think Ms. Englert would like her students betting against each other. That seemed like the opposite of F-U-N.

Gabby crossed her arms and smirked. "Yeah. I figured you'd be too chicken."

"Excuse me?"

"You're chicken because Isabella and Jay and I are better tap dancers than you and Emmie and Rio."

"No way!"

"Way! I've been working extra-hard on my tap lately. And Isabella and Jay are *almost* as good as me. Your team doesn't stand a chance."

Shai stewed and simmered in her head. She felt like doing a mad Hurricane Shai dance.

"Fine! I'll do the bet! Except, the loser has to bring the winner a cupcake every day for a whole *month*!" Shai blurted out.

"Deal!"

"Deal!"

They made it official with a pinkie-swear. Shai smiled so hard that her teeth hurt. She wanted to let Gabby know how sure and confident she was about the Dancy Pants Trio.

But inside, her stomach twisted with worry.

What had she just agreed to? Was it too late for take-backs?

"FYI, my favorite flavor is chocolate with raspberry frosting. So make sure you have lots of those," Gabby said with a hair-flip. "Oh, and FYI, 'FYI' means For Your Information."

Shai glared at Gabby. *Forget about take-backs.*

"FYI, my favorite flavor is lemonade: *lemon with lemon frosting,*" she told Gabby, also with a hair-flip.

The cupcake bet was on!

Lemon   Chocolate
         Raspberry

A Mystery

Shai was trying to do her English homework. Ms. Cremaldi had assigned them to write a short mystery story, and it was due a week from Friday.

Shai's Morkie puppy, Sugar, was sleeping on her lap. The new cat, Sweetiepie, was making a sphinx position on top of Shai's desk and gazing at Sugar with hooded eyes. Sweetiepie used to be called Crabbycakes, but Momma thought that calling her a sweet name might help make her personality less crabby.

It was a dark and stormy night! Shai wrote in her notebook. The notebook was turquoise and covered with fairies and emoji stickers.

She crossed out the first line and wrote: *Once upon a time, a mysterious thing happened!!!!!* She knew that exclamation points always made words more interesting and dramatic. But she crossed out that line too.

Her brain just wasn't focused on story writing. It was focused on the cupcake bet, and it kept flip-flopping back and forth on the matter.

At the moment, her brain was flip-flopping in the direction of "Cancel the bet!!!!!" Because how was Shai going to explain to Emmie and Rio that they absolutely *had* to get a ribbon so she wouldn't lose to Gabby?

Yeah, no pressure, guys, she thought glumly.

But maybe it was no big deal. So what if she lost the bet? Losing was part of life. *Sometimes you win, sometimes you lose,* Daddy often said.

Shai shook her head and huffed out an angry breath. It *was* a big deal. She couldn't lose to Gabby. The girl was just so . . . so . . . so . . . *arrogant,* like she thought she was better than everyone else.

Shai reached over Sweetiepie, dug into a bowl of gummy worms, and plopped one into her mouth. Maybe a snack would help her calm down and come up with a solution to her problem.

But the only thing it did was make her hungry for more gummy worms.

Sighing, Shai headed downstairs. It was almost time for dinner, and Momma and Daddy would not be pleased if she filled up on gummy worms, so she had better put them back.

Grandma Rosa and Aunt Mac-N-Cheese were in the kitchen cooking dinner. Grandma Rosa was Momma's momma and lived around the corner. Aunt Mac-N-Cheese was Momma's sister and lived downtown. Shai knew that Momma was working late at her veterinary clinic and Daddy had taken Samantha for her speech therapy appointment.

Yummy smells came from the kitchen.

Voices came from the kitchen too . . . low, whispery voices.

"We can't tell Annemarie and Shaquille," said Grandma Rosa.

"It'll be our secret," said Aunt Mac-N-Cheese.

Shai scrunched up her forehead. *What couldn't they tell Momma and Daddy?*

Obviously, she had to find out. She popped one last gummy worm into her mouth, for courage, and strolled into the kitchen.

Grandma Rosa was at the stove, stirring something bubbly and steamy. Aunt Mac-N-Cheese was peeling carrots at the sink. Jacobe, who was two, was sitting on the floor with plastic measuring cups and dried pinto beans. The marmalade kitties, Purrball and Furball, were playing cat-soccer with one of the pinto beans.

"What secret?" Shai asked.

Grandma Rosa dropped her ladle into the pot. Aunt Mac-N-Cheese dropped her vegetable peeler. They stared at Shai in surprise.

"Cake," Jacobe muttered. He scooped a cup full of pinto beans and poured them over his head. Purrball and Furball meowed and scattered. Jacobe gave an evil baby cackle.

"What secret?" Shai repeated.

Grandma Rosa picked up a yellow thingamajiggy from the counter. Whatever it was, it was small and flat and papery.

"Oh, hello Shaianne," Grandma Rosa said. She slipped the thingamajiggy into her apron pocket. "Your aunt MacKenzie and I were just—"

"—trying to figure out what to serve for dessert later!" Aunt Mac-N-Cheese finished with a bright smile. "You hungry, sweetpea? Would you like a cup of this delicious soup that Mom made? You can help me with the coleslaw if you'd like. Oh, and there's a nice banana bread baking in the oven!"

"Cake," Jacobe repeated.

Shai narrowed her eyes with suspicion. Grandma Rosa and Aunt Mac-N-Cheese were both actors, which meant that they were good at lying. Not bad-lying, like when a person might say, "I *already* brushed my teeth," but good-lying, as in improvising and pretending. Grandma Rosa used to be a famous stage actor.

Aunt Mac-N-Cheese had studied drama in college and now performed in plays and musicals around the city.

But Shai was also an actor. She planned to be a famous movie star when she grew up. So she could tell when people were improvising and pretending.

"We were trying to decide between brownies and strawberry ice cream. What's your opinion, sweetpea?" Aunt Mac-N-Cheese was saying.

My opinion is that you guys are hiding something, Shai thought.

Well, she could improvise and pretend too. She tapped her chin with her index finger as if she were carefully weighing the choices. "How about brownies tonight and strawberry ice cream tomorrow night?" she suggested.

"Brilliant!" said Aunt Mac-N-Cheese.

"Brilliant!" Grandma Rosa agreed.

Shai definitely had a mystery on her hands—not just a made-up short-story mystery for English class but a *real* mystery. And she was going to solve it!

SCENE 4

The Pajama Meeting

That night, Shai gathered her siblings for a pajama meeting in her room.

Pajama meetings were rare occurrences. Shai called for them only during emergencies and special occasions. The last pajama meeting had taken place about six months ago so they could come up with a present idea for Momma's fortieth birthday. (They had made her a hunormous platter at the ceramics store with all their handprints on it, and Momma

had cried happy tears when she unwrapped it.)

Shai sat on the bed and gazed out at her audience. There was Jacobe in his footie pajamas, drinking milk from his pink sippy cup. Next to him was Samantha in her polka-dotty nightgown, cradling her dragon stuffy, Mr. Firebreath.

At the far end was Jamal, who was still in his basketball clothes from practice earlier. He was in middle school, which meant that he was practically a grown-up, so his bedtime was later than the other kids'. He had brought along his history textbook and was going over it.

The pets had come to the meeting too. Sugar, Patches, Marti, Sandy, and Noodle the Poodle were sitting at attention on the rug. Sweetiepie, Purrball, and Furball were lying on the bed. The only ones missing were Samantha's hamsters, Ham and Ster, and the goldfish, Goldilocks.

"Ahem." Shai cleared her throat. "May I have your attention? I've—"

"Shai-Shai, you forgot to say 'please,'" Samantha cut in.

Shai gave a loud drama sigh. Samantha was the queen of not saying "please" or "thank you." "May I have your attention, *please*? I've called you all here today because we have a mystery to solve. Grandma Rosa and Aunt Mac-N-Cheese are keeping a big, huge secret from Momma and Daddy. We have to find out what it is!"

Jamal glanced up from his history textbook. His new glasses made him look like a very smart bug. "Why can't we just ask them?" he suggested.

"I already tried that. They just pretended like there *was* no secret. But of course there is because I could tell," Shai replied.

Jamal rolled his eyes. "Okay, Nancy Drew.

How do you propose we solve this mystery, then?"

"Mystery, history, blistery, kisstery!" Samantha chanted.

"I'm delighted you asked," Shai said to Jamal.

Shai opened her turquoise notebook. She had written down assignments for everyone.

She tore out the assignment pages and passed them around.

"Jamal, your job is to spy on Grandma Rosa and Aunt Mac-N-Cheese. Jacobe, your job is to help Jamal."

"Cake," Jacobe mumbled. He pulled a brownie crumb out of his hair and put it in his mouth. The dogs trotted over to him and sniffed eagerly at his head. The cats continued lying on the bed and pretended not to notice the dogs.

"Samantha, your job is to find the yellow clue," Shai added.

"Yellow glue?" Samantha repeated.

"*Clue*. Clues help detectives solve mysteries. Like footprints . . . or a handkerchief with initials. Before, in the kitchen, I saw Grandma Rosa put something yellow in her apron pocket. I think she was trying to hide it from me. I need you to find it and bring it to me."

"If I find it, do I win the contest?" Samantha said eagerly.

"This isn't a contest. We're solving a mystery together. Like a detective club. We could call ourselves . . . let's see . . . how about the Spy Squad?"

"Spy Squash!" Jacobe muttered.

Shai uncapped her marker and wrote "The Spy Squad" in her notebook in extra-curly cursive. The Spy Squad. The Dancy Pants Trio. The Cool Books Club. She sure belonged to a lot of clubs and groups!

Someone knocked on the door. Shai sat up very straight.

"Intruders!" she warned the others.

The door opened, and Momma and Daddy peeked in. Jacobe squealed and ran up to Daddy.

"Wow, is this a party?" Daddy asked, scooping Jacobe up in his arms. "Buddy, why does your hair smell like chocolate?"

"Yellow glue!"

Jacobe announced. "Spy Squash!"

Momma eyed Shai's notebook and the assignment pages scattered around. "Hmm, looks like you guys are working on a top-secret project!"

"*No!*" Shai said quickly. "This is *not* a top-secret project! They're, um, helping me write a mystery story for my English homework!"

"We are?" Samantha said, wrinkling her nose.

Momma and Daddy exchanged a glance.

"Oo-kay," Momma said with a laugh. "Let us know if we can help too!"

"Nope, we're good," Shai replied.

"Nope, we're good, *thank you*," Samantha corrected her.

Shai made another loud drama sigh.

Being a detective was not easy!

More Secrets

On Saturday afternoon Shai and Emmie and Rio got together in the Williamses' basement for their first "Singin' in the Rain" rehearsal.

Shai liked the basement, which was mostly for storage except for a big room with a comfy old couch and a ping-pong table. For today's rehearsal, Momma and Daddy had moved the ping-pong table aside and put down a portable wooden dance floor on top of the concrete. The floor used to belong to Aunt Mac-N-Cheese from when she took tap-dancing lessons in high school.

Shai had posted a very official sign on the basement door:

She had added a picture of a T-rex with extra-sharp teeth, for good measure. So far, the sign seemed to be working.

While Emmie and Rio did warm-up

stretches, Shai plopped down on the couch and put on her tap shoes.

"Should we practice just the beginning today? The part with the words?" Rio said, stretching his arms over his head.

"Yes!" Emmie replied. She bent down and touched her toes.

"No!" said Shai. "We should practice the whole thing. The words part and the no-words part and the ending, too."

"But Shai! That's too much for one rehearsal," Emmie complained.

"We have to practice, practice, practice if we're going to w—" Shai stopped herself before she said "win." "If we're going to have fun at Dancing With Kids!" she added quickly. "Come on, let's get started. We have a *lot* to do!"

Emmie raised one eyebrow at Shai. She was

probably wondering why Shai was so insistent. Rio was probably wondering that too.

Shai still hadn't told them about her cupcake bet with Gabby. Of course, she didn't like keeping secrets from her friends. But on the other hand, if she *did* tell, they would probably get mad at her for agreeing to Gabby's bet without asking them first.

Losing the bet was not an option either. Not to Gabby. And to be really honest, Shai *liked* to win. Momma always said she was competitive, just like Momma herself when she was in veterinary school and studied extra-hard to get the highest grades in her class.

So really, the best solution was not telling Emmie and Rio and just making sure they won a ribbon at the competition.

Which meant that they had to be no-mistakes and amazetastic and perfect.

Which meant that Shai had to keep them on track.

Shai stood up and tapped her feet against the wooden floor: *taptaptaptaptap*. Then she opened the music app on Momma's phone, pushed the play button, and took her position. Rio and Emmie took their positions too.

A cheerful song filled the air:

> *I'm singin' in the rain*
> *Just singin' in the rain*

The three of them began dancing the steps that Ms. Englert had taught them. During the first few bars they had the same choreography: step-ball-change to the right . . . step-ball-change to the left . . . repeat seven more times. A step-ball-change to the right meant taking a sideways step with the right foot while lifting onto the ball of the left foot, then putting the left foot behind the right foot. A step-ball-change to the left was the same thing, except starting with the left foot.

As Shai danced, she sideways-spied on Rio and Emmie.

"Arms go the other way!" she snapped at Rio. "Toe heel turn!" she snapped at Emmie.

Both Rio *and* Emmie shot her one-eyebrow looks.

They were just beginning to rehearse the next section when Shai heard mysterious footsteps on the basement stairs. Was it Jamal? Or Jacobe? The most likely suspect was Samantha.

Shai hit the stop button on the phone. *"Samanthayouareinsomuchtrouble!"* she yelled.

"It's me, Shaianne, honey!"

Grandma Rosa appeared on the landing. She held a tray in her hands. A magazine was tucked under one arm.

Shai had not made any progress on solving the mystery of Grandma Rosa and Aunt Mac-N-Cheese's secret since the pajama meeting. She knew that her siblings were busy with their assignments—or she hoped so, anyway. She, too, was busy, making her brain try to figure out what the secret might be.

Grandma Rosa set down the tray and the magazine on a crate. The magazine was called *Perfect Parties*. On the tray were a plate of banana nut muffins and three glasses of iced tea with fresh mint.

"I thought you children would enjoy some snacks," she said. "This is peach iced tea, and the mint is from my herb garden. How is your dance routine coming along?"

"Great!" Shai replied with a smile.

"Uh-huh." Emmie didn't smile.

"Yup." Rio didn't smile either.

Shai frowned. Why were Emmie and Rio acting all grumpy? But maybe they were just hangry (which meant you were angry because you were hungry).

Everyone sat down on the comfy old couch.

Grandma Rosa told a funny story about the time she had to do a tap-dance routine for a Broadway play.

Something caught Shai's eye. On the cover of Grandma Rosa's magazine was a picture of a beautiful cake decorated with real flowers. Next to the photo were the words: PERFECTION IN FIVE EASY STEPS!

Hmmm, Shai thought, perking up.

Perfection meant being perfect. And perfect was exactly what her trio needed to be in order to win a ribbon at Dancing With Kids.

Could Grandma Rosa's magazine help with that?

SCENE 6

Five Easy Steps

Shai sat at the kitchen table and kicked her heels against the rung of the chair. She blew on her hot chocolate with extra marshmallows and took a tiny sip, being careful not to drip on her Sunday church dress that Aunt Mac-N-Cheese had made for her out of green silk and ivory lace.

Shai was reading the article called "Perfection in Five Easy Steps!" in Grandma Rosa's magazine. Grandma Rosa had left it lying

around on the counter with a bunch of color-
ful stickies attached to the pages.

But the article
wasn't about how
to be perfect. It
was about how to
throw a perfect party.

Still, the advice
might work for a dance
competition, right?

Shai reached for
her notebook and pen.
Flipping to a blank
page, she began copy-
ing the article into her
notebook . . . except
that she replaced the
word "party" with
"dance routine":

PERFECTION IN 5 EASY STEPS!

1.   Set clear goals for your perfect ~~party~~.

dance routine

2.   Be a leader! Put together a team you can

trust and make sure they understand your directions.

3.   Watch videos of perfect ~~parties~~ dance

routines and learn from their examples.

4.   Make your perfect ~~party~~ dance routine a

priority. Your hard work will pay off in the end!

5.   When the big day comes . . . have fun!

Shai read over what she had written down and nodded to herself. She liked all the advice, especially number three about watching videos. She would ask Jamal to help her find some dance videos on the family computer. She, Emmie, and Rio could watch them at their next rehearsal.

"Ahoy!"

Shai glanced up from her notebook. Samantha stood in the kitchen doorway. She had changed out of her own Sunday dress. She now wore a pink ballet tutu over Jamal's old pirate costume, which included a dangly eye patch and a shoulder parrot.

"Are you a pirate?" Shai asked.

"Aye, aye, matey!" replied Samantha. She held up a black loot sack with a skull-and-crossbones sign on it.

"Is that your pirate treasure?"

"Aye, aye, matey!" Samantha pirate-swaggered up to the table and dumped the contents of the loot sack.

Shai surveyed the pile. There was a yellow marble. A

☆ 53 ☆

yellow crayon. Some yellow Lego pieces. A spool of yellow thread. A yellow doll dress. A yellow scarf. A yellow toothbrush. One yellow mitten.

"Um . . . what are these?" Shai asked.

"These are the yellow glues! I solved the mystery, matey!" Samantha announced.

"Oh!"

Shai didn't know how to tell her little sister that none of these were clues. Then she remembered step number two in Grandma Rosa's article: *Be a leader! Put together a team you can trust and make sure they understand your directions.* The advice could work for mystery solving too.

"Thanks, Samantha. Could you keep looking, though? I think what Grandma Rosa put in her pocket was flat. Like maybe a yellow card or a yellow piece of paper."

"Arrrgh," Samantha said, pouting.

Jamal came into the kitchen just then. Jacobe

trailed after him, dragging a rubber ducky on a yarn leash. Sweetiepie jumped onto the table and pawed at Samantha's yellow marble. She knocked it to the floor, and Purrball and Furball chased after it.

"Are Momma and Daddy back yet?" Jamal asked Shai.

"They took the dogs for a walk. Then they're picking up some pizzas at the restaurant," Shai replied. Daddy owned a neighborhood pizza restaurant called the Super Slice. "How's your detective assignment going? Did you spy on Grandma Rosa and Aunt Mac-N-Cheese yet?"

"Well, Jacobe and I just saw them in the backyard," Jamal said.

"Did they say anything mysterious?" Shai asked.

"They were talking about Grandma Rosa's house. They said something about getting it ready."

"Ready for what?"

Jamal shrugged. "Dunno. Then Aunt Mac-N-Cheese mentioned Jacksonville."

"Jacksonville?"

Jacksonville was a city in Florida. It was about a five-hour drive from Atlanta. Last year Daddy's parents, Grandpa Ben and Grandma Marie, had moved to Jacksonville, to a retirement home by the ocean. Shai and her family, including Grandma Rosa and Aunt Mac-N-Cheese, had visited them at Thanksgiving time.

"Did they say any other mysterious things?" Shai asked Jamal.

"Uh-huh," Jamal said, lowering his voice. He glanced around as if to make sure no one was listening. "They said that the stolen treasure is buried under the magical cauliflower tree! Its exact location shall be revealed during the next full moon!"

"Ha-ha, very funny," Shai muttered.

Jacobe tried to grab Sweetiepie's tail. "Cake!"

"Her name isn't Crabbycakes anymore. It's Sweetiepie," Shai reminded her little brother.

Jacobe chased Sweetiepie down the hall. Jamal went over to the refrigerator to find a snack. Samantha stuffed a yellow paper napkin into her black loot bag.

Shai's mind churned.

Jacksonville, Florida.

Grandma Rosa's house.

The yellow clue.

What did this all add up to? What, exactly, was Grandma Rosa and Aunt Mac-N-Cheese's big secret?

Jacksonville, Florida

Yellow Clue

Grandma Rosa's House

Confession Time

"Did you finish *Little Women* yet?" Emmie asked Shai as they walked into school on Monday morning. "Who do you like best, Jo or Beth or Meg or Amy? And what do you think 'hobbledehoy' means? Isn't that the awesomest word ever?"

"Hmm?"

Shai was lost in thought. Never mind "hobbledehoy"... she was still mulling over what Jacksonville and the other clues might mean.

She was also worried about the Dancing With Kids competition. It was happening in exactly three weeks and five days, and the Dancy Pants Trio had rehearsed only once. They still had a long way to go to achieve "perfect"!

Shai tried to remember the words she had written in her notebook yesterday. *Watch videos of perfect dance routines and learn from their examples. Make your perfect dance routine a priority. Your hard work will pay off in the end!*

Emmie elbowed her. "Helloooo? Earth to Shai!"

"What? Hey, so I think we should add extra rehearsals this week. And next week too. And the week after that. Maybe we should rehearse every day? My parents said we can keep using the basement if we want. We have to make our dance routine our priority. Our hard work will pay off in the end! Oh, and I found videos of dance routines that I want to show you guys. We can learn from their examples!"

Emmie put her hands on her hips. "Seriously?"

"Huh?"

"This dance competition is supposed to be fun. That's what Ms. Englert said. Why are you making it so un-fun?"

Shai put her hands on her hips too. "What do you mean? This *is* fun."

"Hardly!"

Emmie's cheeks flushed red all the way to her ears. This only happened when she was embarrassed or mad. In this case, it was definitely mad.

Shai sighed.

The two girls crossed the lobby. A group of second graders hurried by with their violin and cello cases. Principal DiMarco stood outside his office and wished everyone a good morning as they passed by.

"Good morning, Shai! Good morning, Emmie! Did you girls have a nice weekend?" he called out.

"Hobbledehoy!" Shai replied. She thought that might cheer Emmie up.

But Emmie just frowned.

Shai frowned too. She really wanted to win the bet against Gabby. Still, she didn't know how to make their dance routine perfect without upsetting Emmie—and Rio, too.

On top of that, Shai felt squirmy-uncomfortable about continuing to keep the bet a secret from her friends, especially her bestie-best friend.

She took a deep courage breath. *Time to fix this.*

"Okay, Em. I need to tell you something."

Emmie raised one eyebrow. "What about?"

"Shane! Emmie!"

Shai turned and saw Gabby coming toward them. She wasn't walking, though; she was doing a move called a running flap, which went *brush-step, brush-step, brush-step, brush-step, brush-step.* It was a pretty good running flap, considering that Gabby was wearing sneakers and not tap shoes. Isabella and Jay trailed after Gabby, carrying her backpack and lunch bag, which had gold movie-star stars on them.

Gabby slowed down to a halt and twirled smoothly. "*Soooo.* How's your 'Singin' in the Rain' routine?" she asked.

Shai gulped.

Before either she or Emmie could answer, Gabby plunged on. "Yeah, that's what I thought. I think I've got this bet in the bag. Of course, I'll share the prize with you both," she told Isabella and Jay. "I'll take, like, twenty cupcakes, and you can split the rest. That's fair, right?"

Emmie's confused glance bounced between Gabby and Shai. "What bet? What prize? What cupcakes?"

"Ohmigosh, Shane. You didn't *tell* her?" Gabby exclaimed. "Why not? Did you want to keep all the cupcakes for yourself? That's

kind of greedy, isn't it? Doesn't matter, though, because you guys are totally not going to win! Buh-bye!"

Gabby waved and started doing another running flap in the direction of the homeroom hall. Isabella and Jay hurried after her.

"What was Gabby talking about, Shai?" Emmie asked. She seemed *really* mad now.

"I was just about to tell you."

"Tell me what?"

Shai took another deep courage breath and explained about the cupcake bet.

When she was done, Emmie just shook her head.

"I can't believe you made this bet with Gabby without asking Rio and me first!"

"I know. I'm really, really sorry. Double-triple-quadruple sorry. But now that you know, you can help me make our routine perfect so we can win the bet! Rio can help too, after we tell him!"

Emmie shook her head again.

"Em?"

"I need to go see Mr. Yee before homeroom. About orchestra. I'll see you later."

With that, Emmie turned on her heel and walked away.

Shai's lower lip quivered. Her brain was full of confusion. Why was Emmie still mad? Shai had confessed *and* apologized.

But maybe Emmie would change her mind after she'd had a chance to think about it.

Or maybe she wouldn't.

Then what?

Worst Dancer Ever

Shai was curled up on the living room couch with the remote control in one hand and her favorite blue Polar Blast drink in the other. Sugar lay at her feet, blinking at the TV screen.

Tonight was supposed to be the Dancy Pants Trio's third rehearsal. But Emmie and Rio had both said they needed to finish their short mystery stories for Ms. Cremaldi, which were due on Friday.

Shai needed to finish her short story too.

But she wasn't in the mood to do homework right now. She was in the mood to figure out how to win the cupcake bet . . . and how to win back Emmie and Rio.

Rio was siding with Emmie about the bet. At their last rehearsal he had told Shai, nicely, to chill out and not be so obsessed with winning. He'd reminded her that Ms. Englert wanted Dancing With Kids to be a fun experience plus a learning experience for future competitions.

But why couldn't DWK be a fun experience *plus* a learning experience *plus* a beating-Gabby experience?

Surely Rio and Emmie would come around. . . .

I'm singin' in the rain
Just singin' in the rain

On the television, three members of the Atlanta
Dance Ensemble danced to the song. "Ensemble"
was a fancy Europe word for "group." The three
dancers were all grown-ups. They wore raincoats
and rain hats and rain boots with metal taps on
them, and they carried folded-up umbrellas.
They did running flaps across the stage. They did

single wings and double wings and buffalos.

Jamal had found this video for Shai, and she had watched it over and over again. Grandma Rosa's magazine was right. It *did* help to watch videos of other people's perfect examples. Shai was learning so much from the way the three dancers moved together. They made everything look so fun and energetic and joyous.

The video had also inspired Shai to change

the choreography in the no-words part of the song. Not just change, but make them way harder, like in the video. The new steps were sure to impress the Dancing With Kids judges and earn the Dancy Pants Trio a ribbon!

Okay, so maybe these weren't the steps Ms. Englert had taught them. But wouldn't she be impressed that Shai had "displayed leadership" and challenged her team to do better, think bigger? Shai hit the pause button, then rewind, then play. Standing up, she watched the no-words part carefully and tried to repeat the grown-up dancers' complicated steps. Her flip-flops slapped noisily against the floor, and her ankles wobbled. She knew she wasn't supposed to tap-dance without proper shoes; she could hurt herself. But it was just for a few minutes, and besides, Gabby had done running flaps in her sneakers in the school lobby, right?

Shai hit pause and rewind and play again.

Running flap across the stage . . . single wing to the right . . . single wing to the left . . . double wing.

Shai nodded to herself. Then she launched into a running flap across the living room floor.

Sugar leaped up from her cozy TV-watching spot and ran alongside Shai, barking.

"I know, girl. These steps are super-difficult!" Shai said breathlessly.

Shai stopped in the middle of the living room and kicked up her heels to the right for the single wing. *Yes!* It was a perfect single wing.

Then she kicked up her heels to the left for the other single wing . . .

. . . except that her right foot twisted as she landed. Not good-twisted but bad-twisted.

Pain seared through her right ankle.

"Owwwww!" Shai yelled.

She sank down to the floor and massaged
her ankle, willing the pain to go away. Her eyes
were swimming with tears. What had she done?

Sugar ran in circles around Shai, barking and
barking. Patches and Noodle trotted into the

living room and began circling and barking too.

Momma rushed in from the kitchen. "Why are the dogs making such a . . . Shai, sweetie, are you okay? What happened?"

"I, um . . ."

Momma knelt down and inspected Shai's ankle, which was starting to swell up.

"Oh, honey bunny. It looks like a sprain. Let's get some ice on that right away."

"Are you *sure* it's a sprain?"

"I'm a doctor, remember? An animal doctor, but still. I'm going to go and grab an ice pack, and an elastic bandage, too."

"O-okay."

On the TV the "Singin' in the Rain" song slowly faded. The three dancers opened their umbrellas, twirled, and bowed with happy smiles. The audience clapped and clapped.

Tears spilled down Shai's cheeks. Forget

winning the cupcake bet. . . . Now she probably wouldn't be able to perform in the Dancing With Kids competition at all. Not with an injury like this.

And her ankle hurt like crazy.

Why had she done those crazy-hard dance steps in her flip-flops?

She deserved a ribbon. A ribbon for Worst Dancer Ever.

Winning and Losing

Shai didn't go to school the next day. She lay in her bed with her right foot bandaged up like a mini-mummy and smelling like medicine cream. The foot was propped up on a pile of fluffy pillows with an ice pack wedged against it.

Momma and Daddy were at work. Jamal and Samantha were in school. Grandma Rosa had come over to watch her and Jacobe for the day. Shai could hear them downstairs, stomping and dancing to the "Head, Shoulders, Knees, and Toes" song.

Blah.

Shai was feeling sorry for herself. Very, *very* sorry. She was stuck at home with her sprained ankle. Momma had taken her to the pediatrician this morning. Dr. Holby had confirmed that Shai's ankle was definitely sprained and that she needed to stay off it for a while. And that if Shai took extra-good care of it, there was a slight chance she could still dance in the Dancing With Kids competition.

Shai knew what "slight" meant. *Small. Tiny. Itty-bitty. Practically zero.*

She might as well give up on the competition right now.

Not to mention . . . she had also managed to make her best friend and her other friend kind of upset with her. *And* she had to break the news to them about not being able to dance.

Could things get any worse?

Sighing, Shai picked up her notebook and opened it to her short mystery story. It was due in English class the day after tomorrow, and she still hadn't finished it. Or rather, she'd written lots of beginnings, but she'd never managed to write any middles or endings. She should work on it now, since she didn't have anything better to do; besides, it might take her mind off her troubles.

Shai tapped her marker against the paper . . . thinking, thinking.

Then she began to write:

THE MYSTERY

OF THE MYSTERIOUS SECRET

By Shai Williams

Once upon a time, there was a girl named Shane. One night she went downstairs for dinner and heard her grandma and aunt having a mysterious conversation!

"We can't tell Shane's momma or daddy!" Grandma said.

"It'll be our secret!" Auntie said.

Shane saw Grandma hide something yellow in her apron pocket!

Later, Shane's brother said that he heard Grandma and Auntie talking about Grandma's house and about Jacksonville, Florida!

Dun dun dun!

Shai paused to look up "Jacksonville" in the atlas to make sure she had spelled it right. She had.

What was their mysterious secret? Why couldn't they tell Shane's momma and daddy . . . or anyone else?

There was a knock on the door. Shai slapped her notebook shut. "Come in!"

Grandma Rosa entered, carrying a tray. She placed it on the bed next to Shai.

"The little man went down for his nap. I brought you some lunch."

"Thanks, Grandma Rosa." Shai slid her notebook under the blanket.

"It's carrot-ginger soup. There's extra honey-butter for the corn muffins. How's that ankle feeling, Shaianne?"

"Blah."

"I'm sorry."

Shai picked up a corn muffin and slathered it with honey-butter. Grandma Rosa wiped her hands on her apron and perched on the edge of the bed.

"So . . . a little bird told me that you made a bet with your classmate about a dance competition. And that you were pushing yourself and your trio quite hard to make sure you win a ribbon at the competition," Grandma Rosa said.

Shai almost spit out her corn muffin. "*What? Who told you that?*"

"Emmie. Don't be angry with her. She came by this morning so the two of you could walk to school together. You were at the doctor's office with your momma. That's when she told me everything."

Shai fumed inside. She wasn't angry with

Emmie. She was angry with herself. Why had she gotten so caught up in Gabby's stupid bet?

"I gave Emmie the bad news about your ankle," Grandma Rosa went on. "She was real worried about you. She asked if she could come by after school and bring you some beef jerky and gummy worms from B & L's Market."

"She did?"

"She most certainly did."

Grandma Rosa plumped the pillows under Shai's foot. She rearranged the ice pack.

"Shaianne, it's okay to want to win," she said gently. "It's a fine quality in you, and it will help you succeed in life. You know, when I was growing up, girls weren't supposed to be competitive—only boys. Competitiveness was thought to be unladylike and bad manners. Which of course is a bunch of bananas. So it's wonderful to see young women like you who not only are competitive but work very hard to be the best they can be."

Shai brightened. "Really?"

"Yes! But it's important to remember that *not* winning is fine too. A person can't win *all* the time. Losing is okay; it's how we learn and grow. It's also an opportunity to be gracious to the winners."

Shai tried to imagine being gracious to Gabby. *Ugh.*

"But I want you to ask yourself: Why do you want to win that ribbon and that bet so much?" Grandma Rosa asked. "Is it because you want to be the best you can be? Or is it because you can't stand the thought of losing to your classmate . . . Gabby, is it?"

It was like Grandma Rosa could read her mind.

Grandma Rosa patted Shai's knee. "Shaianne,

☆ 84 ☆

you are the smartest eight-year-old I know. You'll figure this out. In the meantime, eat that soup before it gets cold. I'm going to go catch up on my emails."

She rose to her feet. As she did, something fell out of her apron pocket and landed on the bed.

Something yellow. And small. And flat.

Shai sat up eagerly. It was the yellow clue!

Grandma Rosa quickly reached down, but Shai scooped it up first.

Shai turned it over in her hand. It was a yellow index card.

A bunch of words and numbers were written on it in hasty, scribbly cursive. Shai could make out *beach* and *vista* and a 9 and a 3 and . . .

Grandma Rosa plucked the card from Shai. "I'll take that."

"What is it?"

"An important phone number."

"But—"

Grandma Rosa slipped the card back into her apron pocket and turned toward the door. "I think I hear the little man. Must've been the shortest nap in history! Let me know if you need anything, honey."

With that, she was gone.

Shai twisted her face into a thinking expression. Her brain went into detective mode.

She hadn't heard Jacobe make a peep.

And Grandma Rosa had acted double-triple-quadruple secretive just now.

Whose phone number was on the card?

Shai picked up her notebook and opened it to "The Mystery of the Mysterious Secret."

The story wasn't over yet.

SCENE 10

Together Again

Shai stopped working on her short story around four o'clock. She finally had a middle. Now all she needed was an ending.

The doorbell rang downstairs. The dogs began crazy-barking, and Grandma Rosa said something to someone in a cheery voice.

A moment later, two familiar faces peered into Shai's room. Emmie and Rio!

"Hobbledehoy! I come bearing gummy worms," Emmie said, holding up a paper bag.

"And I've got beef jerky," Rio said, holding up another bag. "We went to B & L's Market."

"Aww! You *guys!*" Shai grinned from ear to ear. It was so nice to see her friends.

Emmie gave Shai a big hug. "I'm sorry about your ankle. And I'm sorry we had a fight."

"Me too!" Shai said, hugging her back.

Rio pointed to Shai's ankle. "Does it hurt a lot?"

"Yup. Dr. Holby said I have to RICE it for a bunch of days."

"Rice, like the food?" Rio asked, confused.

"R-I-C-E. It's doctor language for Rest, Ice, Compression, and Elevation. Compression means the squeezy bandage, and elevation means the pillows," Shai explained.

"*Then* will you be all better? Will you be able to ..." Emmie hesitated. "Will you be able to dance with us at DWK?"

Shai looked away. "Um, I'm not sure. Probably not. But maybe."

"Maybe is good," Rio said with a smile.

Emmie nodded. "'Maybe is great! Hey, I have an idea. Rio and I can come over every day and rehearse here. You can watch us and take notes and give us advice and stuff. And when your ankle's healed, you can dance with us."

"Really?" Shai's heart swelled with hope.

"You guys don't want to be the Dancy Pants Duo instead?"

"Nope," said Rio.

"Never ever," Emmie added.

"Even though I made that bet with Gabby? And I was super-duper strict?"

"You weren't that strict!" Emmie said, offering Shai a gummy worm.

"Yeah. Just *kind of* strict," Rio joked.

They all laughed.

Shai handed in her short mystery story later that week. She wasn't 100 percent happy with the ending, though. She hadn't been able to figure out Grandma Rosa and Aunt Mac-N-Cheese's secret in real life, so she'd had to improvise an ending—an ending having to do with a stolen treasure buried under a magical cauliflower tree.

In any case, the Spy Squad's mystery solving faded into the background as Shai focused on healing her ankle and preparing for the competition.

For the next few weeks she walked on crutches . . . then walked without the crutches . . . then started to dance a little . . . then started to dance a lot. Emmie and Rio

came over every day to rehearse. At first Shai just watched. Eventually she was able to join in.

Two days before DWK, Dr. Holby gave Shai the official all-clear to compete.

"Don't push yourself, though. Just relax and have fun! And if your ankle starts hurting at all, make sure you stop," she advised.

When the big day finally arrived, Shai and her classmates boarded the school bus that would take them to the Robinson Arena. As Shai sat down in the front row, she thought about Dr. Holby's words. She set her dance bag on the floor and wiggled her ankle. She rotated it clockwise and counterclockwise. No pain. So far, so good!

Emmie scooted in next to her. She unzipped her dance bag, pulled out a pair of gray leg warmers, and stuffed them back in. She squirmed and fidgeted. "Are you nervous? I'm nervous," she said.

"Nah." Shai giggled. "Actually, I lied. I'm super-nervous. I missed so many rehearsals."

"Don't worry. You looked amazetastic at our run-through yesterday. And if you forget your steps . . . just improvise!"

"Yup, that's the plan."

"Go, Dancy Pants Trio!" Rio cheered as he boarded the bus. He tossed his dance bag onto the seat across the aisle, then reached over and high-fived Shai and Emmie.

Gabby stepped onto the bus after Rio. She gave Shai a sideways glance as she walked by. She hadn't said a word about the cupcake bet since Shai sprained her ankle. Shai wondered: Was the bet still on? Was Gabby still expecting to win?

But really, it didn't matter anymore. Shai would do her best today at the competition. So would Emmie and Rio. And they would get a ribbon or not. If she had to bake cupcakes for Gabby, so be it. In the end, all that mattered was that Shai was dancing again . . . and that the three of them were dancing *together*. A trio. A team.

Ms. Englert counted heads, and then the bus took off. Thirty minutes later they pulled up in front of the Robinson Arena, and everyone got out.

Shai stood on the sidewalk and blinked up at the hunormous silver building before her. Somehow the place looked even more massive than when Momma and Daddy had brought the family to see the women's basketball championship. She couldn't believe she and her friends were dancing here today! And in front

of an audience and TV cameras, too!

More buses pulled up, and more people spilled out onto the sidewalk. Dozens of boys and girls paraded past with their dance bags. Some ballet-walked with their feet turned out slightly in V shapes; some did twirls and jumps and sashays. Matching team jackets created waves of color: a wave of gold (Dalton Dance Academy), a wave of red (Big Apple School of Ballet), a wave of royal blue (Fancy Feet Dance Studio), and so on. Many of the girls had put on performance makeup and styled their hair in tight buns or high ponytails.

Inside, the lobby was crammed wall-to-wall with more dancers, their teachers, and their coaches. Ms. Englert registered all the Sweet Auburn kids at one of the long tables staffed by volunteers.

Then their group proceeded into the main

auditorium to find their seats. The space was beyond hunormous. Shai and the others were like ants inside a football stadium. Audience members were beginning to filter in. A TV crew was setting up lights and cameras near the stage.

Shai's nervous feeling swelled inside her. She tried to do some yoga breaths, which was a calm-down trick that Ms. Englert had taught them. But the nervous feeling wouldn't go away.

Emmie hooked her arm through Shai's. "This is *not* fun. This is scary," she whispered.

"I know. My stomach wants to throw up."

"Mine too."

The two friends huddled close as they followed Ms. Englert to their assigned seats. Shai began yoga-breathing again. Emmie yoga-breathed with her.

Then Rio caught up to them and hooked his arm through Shai's other arm.

The three of them yoga-breathed together.

Is the Dancy Pants Trio ready? Shai wondered.

Onstage!

"And now we have our next contestants in the Tap Small Group category. Please welcome Rio Garcia, Emmie Harper, and Shaianne Williams, who will be performing 'Singin' in the Rain'!"

The master-of-ceremonies man's voice boomed over the speakers, and the audience broke into loud applause. Shai barely noticed that he had pronounced her name "Shy-Anne" instead of "Shay-Anne." As she, Rio, and Emmie walked onto the stage, all she could think about was the terror that filled her brain and heart and every other part of her. They didn't belong here. *She* didn't belong here. She had no business competing in a national dance competition. She had barely made it through "I Wish" at the community center four years ago.

"Break a leg," Rio whispered to Shai and Emmie as they took their positions in the center of the stage.

"Actually, it's 'break an egg,'" Shai whispered back. "Break an egg" was her and Emmie's private, personal version of "break a leg," which was "good luck" in dancer–musician–actor language.

"Yeah. Break an egg, guys," Emmie added.

The familiar music sang out over the speakers:

I'm singin' in the rain
Just singin' in the rain

Shai began to dance. *Step-ball-change to the right . . . step-ball-change to the left . . . repeat seven more times.* The glare of the stage lights made the rest of the auditorium barely visible. She knew that the judges were out there, and all the dancers from the other schools and studios, and the audience members, including her whole entire family. She knew, too, that

the TV camera people were filming.

But after a while she forgot about them. She was thinking about the video of the Atlanta Dance Ensemble that she had watched over and over again. What she remembered about those dancers now was not how hard their chore-ography had been or how expertly they had performed their steps. What she remembered was how happily and joyously and energeti-cally they had moved together, like they were having the most fun they'd ever had in their lives.

Shai closed her eyes for a moment and felt that happiness and joy and energy too. Her feet were tapping like crazy . . . her arms were swinging this way and that . . . and her body was leaping and twirling through the air. She was in control and not in control at the same time.

And when Shai opened her eyes, she saw that Emmie and Rio were right there with her. They all grinned at each other as they tapped and whirled and jumped in rhythm . . . and sometimes not in rhythm, which was okay, because being perfect wasn't the point.

The song slowed and faded. Shai's footsteps slowed and faded too.

When the music stopped, the audience burst into applause. Shai and Emmie and Rio grabbed each other's hands and took their bows.

"That was amazetastic," Shai said to her friends as she smiled at the audience.

"Amazetastic," Emmie agreed.

"Yeah, that," Rio added.

They bowed again and tapped off the stage.

Afterward they sat together in the audience and watched the rest of the dances. Shai had to admit that the dancers from the other schools and studios were pretty incredible. She, Emmie, and Rio got to watch most of their classmates' dances too. Shai especially loved Ezra, Nya, and Sarah's ballet, "Dance of the Flowers," and Glenn, Garrett, and Molly's contemporary dance, "Circle of Life."

They also got to watch Gabby, Isabella, and Jay's tap number. Their trio was really good. And their choreography included lots of difficult steps, like double wings and buffalos.

Later the judges announced the ribbons in each category.

The Sweet Auburn School got two ribbons: one for Gabby, Isabella, and Jay's trio, which got third place in their category, and one for Ezra, Nya, and Sarah's trio, which also got third place in their category.

Everyone gathered around the six winners to congratulate them. Shai took a deep courage breath and marched up to Gabby.

Shai held out her hand. "Congratulations. You did great."

Gabby frowned. "Um . . . but this means you lost, Shane."

"Yeah, I know. I owe you a lot of cupcakes."

"Don't worry about it," Gabby said after a moment. "You had a broken foot or whatever."

"Sprained ankle. And no, it's fine. A bet's a bet."

Shai and Gabby shook hands.

Emmie and Rio came up to them. "I'll help you bake," Emmie said to Shai.

☆ 107 ☆

"Yeah, me too," Rio offered. "Cupcakes are my specialty!"

Grandma Rosa and Aunt Mac-N-Cheese had joined the group. Momma, Daddy, Jamal, Samantha, and Jacobe were right behind.

At the mention of cupcakes, Grandma Rosa and Aunt Mac-N-Cheese turned to each other and winked.

Shai raised one eyebrow—or she tried to, anyway.

Why did they wink at each other?

Shai had put the mystery on hold for the past few weeks. But that wink just now had awakened her detective brain.

It was time to solve the mystery once and for all!

101 Cupcakes

The next morning, Shai went around the corner to Grandma Rosa's house, her notebook tucked under her arm. The air was balmy and warm and smelled like spring flowers. Along the way she passed her next-door neighbors, the Wallises, strolling their new baby. She passed Mrs. Katy walking her hunormous dog, Max.

When Shai got to Grandma Rosa's, she saw Aunt Mac-N-Cheese's car sitting in the driveway. *Good!* She would be able to ask both of them the detective questions that she'd written down in her notebook:

Whose phone number was on the yellow index card?

Why are you getting the house ready? Ready for what?

What's so important about Jacksonville, Florida?

Why did you wink about cupcakes yesterday?

Why can't you tell Momma and Daddy (or anyone else) about your big secret?

Shai headed back to the kitchen door and raised her hand to knock. But just then, she spotted something mysterious through the window.

Grandma Rosa and Aunt Mac-N-Cheese were baking . . . *cupcakes*!

Rows and rows of cupcakes covered the table and counters. There were pink ones and yellow ones and chocolaty ones. Aunt Mac-N-Cheese was opening the oven door and taking out a fresh batch. Grandma Rosa was mixing something in a bowl.

Shai was more confused than ever. Now she understood why Grandma Rosa and Aunt Mac-N-Cheese had winked at each other last night during the cupcake discussion.

But what did cupcakes have to do with the big mystery?

Forget about knocking.…Shai opened the door and marched in. "Aha!" she said in a loud voice.

Grandma Rosa and Aunt Mac-N-Cheese

stopped what they were doing and gazed at her in astonishment.

"Shaianne! What are you doing here?" Grandma Rosa asked.

"I'm here to int—interro—" Shai tried to remember how to pronounce "in-ter-ro-gate," which was detective language for asking detective questions. She'd learned it from a TV show. "What are you guys up to? I know you're keeping a secret!"

Grandma Rosa and Aunt Mac-N-Cheese exchanged a glance.

Then they burst out laughing.

"What's so funny? And why are you baking a billion zillion cupcakes? Are you opening up a cupcake shop in Jacksonville?" Shai guessed.

Grandma Rosa blinked. "Jacksonville? How do you know about Jacksonville?" She wrapped her arm around Shai's shoulders. "You're a clever one, aren't you? I guess we'd best let you in on our secret."

"Definitely!" Shai agreed. She was about to solve the mystery!

Aunt Mac-N-Cheese explained, "You're all coming over here later for Sunday night dinner, right? Except . . . it won't be Sunday night dinner. It's a surprise party for your momma and daddy's twentieth wedding anniversary!"

"Oh!" Shai gasped.

"We're sorry we didn't tell you and the other children before. We really wanted to keep the party top-secret so Momma and Daddy wouldn't find out," Grandma Rosa said. "Oh, and that yellow card? It had the phone number of your grandpa Ben and grandma Marie's retirement home in Jacksonville. We hired a car service to drive them here for the party."

"*Oh!*"

Shai was crazy-surprised by this turn of events. But not as crazy-surprised as Momma and Daddy were going to be tonight!

At five o'clock sharp, Shai, Samantha, Jamal, Jacobe, and Momma and Daddy arrived at Grandma Rosa's front door.

Daddy glanced up and down the street with

a puzzled expression. "Sure are a lot of cars parked here," he remarked.

"Maybe there's a nighttime wedding at the church," Shai improvised.

Momma rang the bell. The door opened, and Grandma Rosa stood there. She was dressed in

a fancy velvet dress, and her eyes were bright with excitement.

"Come in, come in!"

Momma walked in first, then Daddy, then the rest of them.

"Surprise!"

A whole lot of people jumped up from behind couches and chairs and tables and beamed at Momma and Daddy.

Momma and Daddy gazed in shock at the faces in the room and then at each other.

"W-what's this?" Momma stammered.

"I-I don't understand," said Daddy.

"Is this my birthday party?" Samantha spoke up, even though her birthday was months away.

"Cake!" Jacobe cried out—and another piece fell into place as Shai recalled how often

her little brother had been saying that word lately. He, too, must have overheard Grandma Rosa and Aunt Mac-N-Cheese discussing the party.

Then Grandpa Ben and Grandma Marie stepped out from the crowd.

"Happy anniversary, you two lovebirds," Grandma Marie said to Momma and Daddy.

"Hi, son. Hi, Annemarie dear," Grandpa Ben added.

"Mom! Dad!"

There were shrieks and laughter and happy tears as Momma and Daddy rushed up to Grandpa Ben and Grandma Marie and gave them squeezy hugs.

The other guests swarmed around Momma and Daddy with more hugs and

kisses and shouts of congratulations. Shai recognized some people from Daddy's restaurant . . . and other people from Momma's veterinary clinic . . . and tons of friends and neighbors. Ms. Englert was there too; she and Aunt Mac-N-Cheese had been roommates at their college and were still close friends. Emmie had come with her mom and her little twin brothers, Justin and Joseph. The boys rushed up to Jacobe, and the three of them sat down on the floor and covered each other with stickers from Jacobe's sticker book. Also present were Rio and his sister, Celeste, who was in Jamal's class at the middle school.

Grandma Rosa crooked her finger at Shai and Emmie and Rio. They all hurried over to her.

"I need your help in the kitchen. Follow me!"

They trailed after her, weaving through the thick crowd. Once in the kitchen, she gestured grandly at the counter. "MacKenzie and I baked a hundred and one total this morning!"

The 101 cupcakes were arranged on several platters, including the one that Shai and her siblings had made for Momma for her fortieth birthday.

"Your parents will be so delighted," Emmie said to Shai.

Shai giggled. "Yes, these cupcakes are quite splendid!"

Grandma Rosa got a box of matches from a drawer and lit twenty cupcakes—one for each year Momma and Daddy had been married. The candles flickered and glowed in the evening light.

Then she, Shai, Emmie, and Rio carried the platters into the living room, toward the happy, mingled voices of their friends and family.